Superpet!

D1643022

TAMSYN MURRAY

ILLUSTRATED BY LEE WILDISH

Q JF:MUR

J13400X1848

Published by Pearson Education Limited, Edinburgh Gate, Harlow, Essex, CM20 2JE
Registered company number: 872828

www.pearsonschools.co.uk

Text originally published by Simon & Schuster Children's Books in 2010 as part of *Stunt Bunny: Showbiz Sensation.*

Text © Tamsyn Murray 2010
Cover and inside illustrations © 2010 Lee Wildish
Cover design by Bigtop

Interior illustrations and text all used by kind permission from Simon & Schuster Children's Books.

The right of Tamsyn Murray and Lee Wildish to be identified as the author and illustrator of this work respectively has been asserted by them in accordance with sections 77 and 78 of the Copyright, Designs and Patents Act, 1988.

First published 2012

16 15 14 13
10 9 8 7 6 5 4 3

British Library Cataloguing in Publication Data
A catalogue record for this book is available from the British Library

ISBN 978 0 435 07632 0

Printed and bound in Malaysia (CTP-VP)

Acknowledgements
We would like to thank the children and teachers of Bangor Central Integrated Primary School, NI; Barley Hill School, Thame; Bishop Henderson C of E Primary School, Somerset; Brookside Community Primary School, Somerset; Catcott Primary School, Somerset; Cheddington Combined School, Buckinghamshire; Cofton Primary School, Birmingham; Dair House Independent School, Buckinghamshire; Deal Parochial School, Kent; Lawthorn Primary School, North Ayrshire; Newbold Riverside Primary School, Rugby and Windmill Primary School, Oxford for their invaluable help in the development and trialling of the Bug Club resources.

Every effort has been made to contact copyright holders of material reproduced in this book. Any omissions will be rectified in subsequent printings if notice is given to the publisher.

Contents

Chapter 1

Introducing Harriet Houdini

I'll let you into a secret. My name hasn't always been Harriet Houdini.

When Susie Wilson and her dad brought me home from the

pet shop, I was called Flopsy. Have you ever heard anything so ridiculous in your life?

I may have the cutest little bunny ears and the fluffiest grey bunny tail but that doesn't mean I deserve a name like that. After all, I'm not exactly what you'd call an *ordinary* rabbit. The Wilson family first learned this when they opened the box they'd brought me home in and found I wasn't inside.

"She's gone!" exclaimed Susie's mum.

"Where is she?" Susie's voice wobbled.

It was ages before anyone thought of looking in the shed. Even though I had squeezed in tightly between a smelly cat basket and a tatty, old sun-lounger, they found me in the end.

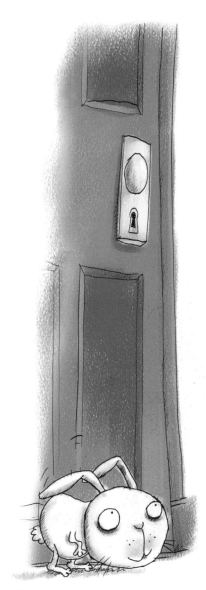

"Flopsy, you bad bunny!"
Susie cried, burying her face in
my soft, grey fur. "Don't ever do
that again."

Just as I was starting to feel
the teeniest bit guilty, Susie's
dad said, "After an escape like
that, we should be calling it
Harry Houdini."

Susie looked confused. "Who?"

"Harry Houdini," he repeated. "He was a famous magician who escaped from all kinds of impossible places, a bit like Flopsy here."

Hands on hips, Susie said, "She's a *girl*. We can't call her Harry."

"How about Harriet, then?"

So that's how I came to be called Harriet Houdini. With a name like that, life was never going to be boring!

Chapter 2

Talent Spotted!

The must-see Saturday night TV show in the Wilson house was *Superpets.* It was hosted by Gloria Goodwood, and starred talented animals from all over the country.

The producers of the show had just launched their *Search for a Superstar* competition. The winner would get a big cash prize and would join the *Superpets* cast. Secretly, I imagined myself auditioning in front of Gloria and the other judges and winning the

Superpets competition.

Of course, I never thought it would actually happen – until the day of our village pet show.

I was sure I was just about to
scoop the Best In Show first
prize. I couldn't believe my
eyes when I saw Gloria herself,
pushing through the crowd
towards my table.

What was a big star like her doing in a tiny village like ours? I wasn't about to waste my chance to impress her, though. Taking a deep breath, I waited until she had a clear view of me. Carefully, I lifted myself onto my back legs and pushed upwards, soaring into a magnificent triple bunny backflip. I landed neatly on the table, ears pointing straight upwards. For a second, no one moved. Then applause burst out all around the tent.

Just as I'd planned, Gloria was hooked. "That's an amazing trick," she said. "Does she do anything else?"

"I don't know if she can do tricks like the pets on your TV show," Susie said, "but she can escape from almost anywhere. That's why we call her Harriet Houdini."

A thoughtful look crossed Gloria's face. "Harriet Houdini? I like it. She's exactly the kind of animal we need on *Superpets*. You should bring her along to our auditions."

She leaned down to study me. "How would you like to be a celebrity, Harriet?"

I didn't need to be asked twice.

Quicker
than you could
say "crunchy
carrots", I
was up on
my back legs
and waving my front paws in
excitement.

"I think that means 'yes'," Gloria said, smiling. "Stick with me, bunny. I'm going to make you a star!"

Chapter 3

Lights, Camera, Action!

It was the day of the *Superpets* final. I had made it through several auditions, and won every stage of the competition.

You wouldn't believe how hot it was in the packed television studio. The lights were so strong I had to have an umbrella, like the ones at the beach on holiday. I even thought about wearing sunglasses but decided not to. I didn't want to be the sort of stuck-up star that no one liked.

I don't mind telling you I was nervous once it was my turn to perform in front of the judges.

We'd seen all kinds of amazing animals, including a hula-hooping chimpanzee and a disco-dancing donkey.

Then, suddenly, the cameras turned on me and the audience went quiet, watching and waiting.

It was the biggest moment of my life and I didn't want to mess it up. What if I did a perfect flip, but fluffed the landing? What if – horror of horrors – I couldn't backflip at all? With my heart beating loudly in my ears, I launched myself into the air.

I needn't have worried.
The *ooohs* and *aaahs* of the
audience as I landed told me
I'd pulled off a fantastic flip
and the little bell I'd rung
with my back paws was a real
crowd-pleaser.

Smiling, Gloria turned to the TV camera. "I'm told that the phone lines have opened and the numbers are on your screen," she said. "If you want to see your favourite pet every week on *Superpets*, vote now!"

I crossed my paws, hoping I'd done enough. If the people at home loved me as much as the studio audience did, the top spot was as good as mine. With a bit of luck, I'd soon be well on my way to becoming Britain's Best Loved Bunny. All I could do now was wait.

Chapter 4

And the Winner is ...

It seemed to take forever for Gloria to announce that the phone lines were closed and the votes had been counted. She lined up all the pets along with our owners on the stage once more and a spotlight shone on each of us.

I sat next to Susie, nibbling my nails nervously. The audience went quiet. This was it – the moment we'd all been waiting for.

"The winner of the *Superpets Search for a Superstar* is ..." Gloria paused and let the dramatic music fill the air. "Harriet Houdini!"

Yes! The crowd erupted into cheers and silver confetti fell from above to cover the stage. As I celebrated with an enormous leap and the rest of the Wilson family rushed onto the stage, Gloria gave Susie a big hug.

"Congratulations, Susie! I'm looking forward to seeing a lot more of this talented rabbit, although I think we might have to rename her." She looked down at me and winked. "How does 'Harriet Houdini – Stunt Bunny' grab you?"

Ooh, I liked the sound of that. I really did. Now that I was the *Superpets* Superstar, my life would never be the same again!